Tacitus

Tacitus on Germany

Outlook

Tacitus

Tacitus on Germany

1. Auflage | ISBN: 978-3-73262-548-2

Erscheinungsort: Frankfurt am Main, Deutschland

Erscheinungsjahr: 2018

Outlook Verlag GmbH, Frankfurt.

Reproduction of the original.

Tacitus

Tacitus on Germany

Outlook

TACITUS ON GERMANY

Translated by Thomas Gordon

INTRODUCTORY NOTE

The dates of the birth and death of Tacitus are uncertain, but it is probable that he was born about 54 A. D. and died after 117. He was a contemporary and friend of the younger Pliny, who addressed to him some of his most famous epistles. Tacitus was apparently of the equestrian class, was an advocate by training, and had a reputation as an orator, though none of his speeches has survived. He held a number of important public offices, and married the daughter of Agricola, the conqueror of Britain, whose life he wrote.

The two chief works of Tacitus, the "Annals" and the "Histories," covered the history of Rome from the death of Augustus to A. D. 96; but the greater part of the "Histories" is lost, and the fragment that remains deals only with the year 69 and part of 70. In the "Annals" there are several gaps, but what survives describes a large part of the reigns of Tiberius, Claudius, and Nero. His minor works, besides the life of Agricola, already mentioned, are a "Dialogue on Orators" and the account of Germany, its situation, its inhabitants, their character and customs, which is here printed.

Tacitus stands in the front rank of the historians of antiquity for the accuracy of his learning, the fairness of his judgments, the richness, concentration, and precision of his style. His great successor, Gibbon, called him a "philosophical historian, whose writings will instruct the last generations of mankind"; and Montaigne knew no author "who, in a work of history, has taken so broad a view of human events or given a more just analysis of particular characters."

The "Germany" is a document of the greatest interest and importance, since it gives us by far the most detailed account of the state of culture among the tribes that are the ancestors of the modern Teutonic nations, at the time when they first came into account with the civilization of the Mediterranean.

TACITUS ON GERMANY

The whole of Germany is thus bounded; separated from Gaul, from Rhoetia and Pannonia, by the rivers Rhine and Danube; from Sarmatia and Dacia by mutual fear, or by high mountains: the rest is encompassed by the ocean, which forms huge bays, and comprehends a tract of islands immense in extent: for we have lately known certain nations and kingdoms there, such as the war discovered. The Rhine rising in the Rhoetian Alps from a summit altogether rocky and perpendicular, after a small winding towards the west, is lost in the Northern Ocean. The Danube issues out of the mountain Abnoba, one very high but very easy of ascent, and traversing several nations, falls by six streams into the Euxine Sea; for its seventh channel is absorbed in the Fenns.

The Germans, I am apt to believe, derive their original from no other people; and are nowise mixed with different nations arriving amongst them: since anciently those who went in search of new dwellings, travelled not by land, but were carried in fleets; and into that mighty ocean so boundless, and, as I may call it, so repugnant and forbidding, ships from our world rarely enter. Moreover, besides the dangers from a sea tempestuous, horrid and unknown, who would relinquish Asia, or Africa, or Italy, to repair to Germany, a region hideous and rude, under a rigorous climate, dismal to behold or to manure [to cultivate] unless the same were his native country? In their old ballads (which amongst them are the only sort of registers and history) they celebrate *Tuisto*, a God sprung from the earth, and *Mannus* his son, as the fathers and founders of the nation. To *Mannus* they assign three sons, after whose names so many people are called; the Ingaevones, dwelling next the ocean; the Herminones, in the middle country; and all the rest, Instaevones. Some, borrowing a warrant from the darkness of antiquity, maintain that the God had more sons, that thence came more denominations of people, the Marsians, Gambrians, Suevians, and Vandalians, and that these are the names truly genuine and original. For the rest, they affirm Germany to be a recent word, lately bestowed: for that those who first passed the Rhine and expulsed the Gauls, and are now named Tungrians, were then called Germans: and thus by degrees the name of a tribe prevailed, not that of the nation; so that by an appellation at first occasioned by terror and conquest, they afterwards chose to be distinguished, and assuming a name lately invented were universally called *Germans*.

They have a tradition that Hercules also had been in their country, and him above all other heroes they extol in their songs when they advance to battle.

Amongst them too are found that kind of verses by the recital of which (by them called *Barding*) they inspire bravery; nay, by such chanting itself they divine the success of the approaching fight. For, according to the different din of the battle they urge furiously, or shrink timorously. Nor does what they utter, so much seem to be singing as the voice and exertion of valour. They chiefly study a tone fierce and harsh, with a broken and unequal murmur, and therefore apply their shields to their mouths, whence the voice may by rebounding swell with greater fulness and force. Besides there are some of opinion, that Ulysses, whilst he wandered about in his long and fabulous voyages, was carried into this ocean and entered Germany, and that by him Asciburgium was founded and named, a city at this day standing and inhabited upon the bank of the Rhine: nay, that in the same place was formerly found an altar dedicated to Ulysses, with the name of his father Laertes added to his own, and that upon the confines of Germany and Rhoetia are still extant certain monuments and tombs inscribed with Greek characters. Traditions these which I mean not either to confirm with arguments of my own or to refute. Let every one believe or deny the same according to his own bent.

For myself, I concur in opinion with such as suppose the people of Germany never to have mingled by inter-marriages with other nations, but to have remained a people pure, and independent, and resembling none but themselves. Hence amongst such a mighty multitude of men, the same make and form is found in all, eyes stern and blue, yellow hair, huge bodies, but vigorous only in the first onset. Of pains and labour they are not equally patient, nor can they at all endure thrift and heat. To bear hunger and cold they are hardened by their climate and soil.

Their lands, however somewhat different in aspect, yet taken all together consist of gloomy forests or nasty marshes; lower and moister towards Noricum and Pannonia; very apt to bear grain, but altogether unkindly to fruit trees; abounding in flocks and herds, but generally small of growth. Nor even in their oxen is found the usual stateliness, no more than the natural ornaments and grandeur of head. In the number of their herds they rejoice; and these are their only, these their most desirable riches. Silver and gold the Gods have denied them, whether in mercy or in wrath, I am unable to determine. Yet I would not venture to aver that in Germany no vein of gold or silver is produced; for who has ever searched? For the use and possession, it is certain they care not. Amongst them indeed are to be seen vessels of silver, such as have been presented to their Princes and Ambassadors, but holden in no other esteem than vessels made of earth. The Germans however adjoining to our frontiers value gold and silver for the purposes of commerce, and are wont to distinguish and prefer certain of our coins. They who live more remote are more primitive and simple in their dealings, and exchange one commodity for another. The money which they like is the old and long known, that indented [with milled edges], or that impressed with a chariot and two horses. Silver too is what they seek more than gold, from no fondness or preference, but because small pieces are more ready in purchasing things cheap and common.

Neither in truth do they abound in iron, as from the fashion of their weapons may be gathered. Swords they rarely use, or the larger spear. They carry javelins or, in their own language, *framms*, pointed with a piece of iron short and narrow, but so sharp and manageable, that with the same weapon they can fight at a distance or hand to hand, just as need requires. Nay, the horsemen also are content with a shield and a javelin. The foot throw likewise weapons missive, each particular is armed with many, and hurls them a mighty space, all naked or only wearing a light cassock. In their equipment they show no ostentation; only that their shields are diversified and adorned with curious colours. With coats of mail very few are furnished, and hardly upon any is seen a headpiece or helmet. Their horses are nowise signal either in fashion or in fleetness; nor taught to wheel and bound, according to the practice of the Romans: they only move them forward in a line, or turn them right about, with such compactness and equality that no one is ever behind the rest. To one who considers the whole it is manifest, that in their foot their principal strength lies, and therefore they fight intermixed with the motions and engagements of the cavalry. So that the infantry are elected from amongst the most robust of their youth, and placed in front of the army. The number to be sent is also ascertained, out of every village *an hundred*, and by this very name they continue to be called at home, *those of the hundred band*: thus what was at first no more than a number, becomes thenceforth a title and distinction of honour. In arraying their army, they divide the whole into distinct battalions formed sharp in front. To recoil in battle, provided you return again to the attack, passes with them rather for policy than fear. Even when the combat is no more than doubtful, they bear away the bodies of their slain. The most glaring disgrace that can befall them, is to have quitted their shield; nor to one branded with such ignominy is it lawful to join in their sacrifices, or to enter into their assemblies; and many who had escaped in the day of battle, have hanged themselves to put an end to this their infamy.

In the choice of kings they are determined by the splendour of their race, in that of generals by their bravery. Neither is the power of their kings unbounded or arbitrary: and their generals procure obedience not so much by the force of their authority as by that of their example, when they appear enterprising and brave, when they signalise themselves by courage and prowess; and if they surpass all in admiration and pre-eminence, if they surpass all at the head of an army. But to none else but the Priests is it allowed to exercise correction, or to inflict bonds or stripes. Nor when the Priests do this, is the same considered as a punishment, or arising from the orders of the general, but from the immediate command of the Deity, Him whom they believe to accompany them in war. They therefore carry with them when going to fight, certain images and figures taken out of their holy groves. What proves the principal incentive to their valour is, that it is not at random nor by the fortuitous conflux of men that their troops and pointed battalions are formed, but by the conjunction of whole families, and tribes of relations. Moreover, close to the field of battle are lodged all the nearest and most interesting pledges of nature. Hence they hear the doleful howlings of their wives, hence the cries of their tender infants. These are to each particular the witnesses whom he most reverences and dreads; these yield him the praise which affect him most. Their wounds and maims they carry to their mothers, or to their wives, neither are their mothers or wives shocked in telling, or in sucking their bleeding sores. Nay, to their husbands and sons whilst engaged in battle, they administer meat and encouragement.

In history we find, that some armies already yielding and ready to fly, have been by women restored, through their inflexible importunity and entreaties, presenting their breasts, and showing their impending captivity; an evil to the Germans then by far most dreadful when it befalls their women. So that the spirit of such cities as amongst their hostages are enjoined to send their damsels of quality, is always engaged more effectually than that of others. They even believe them endowed with something celestial and the spirit of prophecy. Neither do they disdain to consult them, nor neglect the responses which they return. In the reign of the deified Vespasian, we have seen *Veleda* for a long time, and by many nations, esteemed and adored as a divinity. In times past they likewise worshipped *Aurinia* and several more, from no complaisance or effort of flattery, nor as Deities of their own creating.

Of all the Gods, Mercury is he whom they worship most. To him on certain stated days it is lawful to offer even human victims. Hercules and Mars they appease with beasts usually allowed for sacrifice. Some of the Suevians make likewise immolations to *Isis*. Concerning the cause and original of this foreign sacrifice I have found small light; unless the figure of her image formed like a galley, show that such devotion arrived from abroad. For the rest, from the grandeur and majesty of beings celestial, they judge it altogether unsuitable to hold the Gods enclosed within walls, or to represent them under any human likeness. They consecrate whole woods and groves, and by the names of the Gods they call these recesses; divinities these, which only in contemplation and mental reverence they behold.

To the use of lots and auguries, they are addicted beyond all other nations. Their method of divining by lots is exceeding simple. From a tree which bears fruit they cut a twig, and divide it into two small pieces. These they distinguish by so many several marks, and throw them at random and without order upon a white garment. Then the Priest of the community, if for the public the lots are consulted, or the father of a family if about a private concern, after he has solemnly invoked the Gods, with eyes lifted up to heaven, takes up every piece thrice, and having done thus forms a judgment according to the marks before made. If the chances have proved forbidding, they are no more consulted upon the same affair during the same day; even when they are inviting, yet, for confirmation, the faith of auguries too is tried. Yea, here also is the known practice of divining events from the voices and flight of birds. But to this nation it is peculiar, to learn presages and admonitions divine from horses also. These are nourished by the State in the same sacred woods and grooves, all milk-white and employed in no earthly labour. These yoked in the holy chariot, are accompanied by the Priest and the King, or the Chief of the community, who both carefully observed his actions and neighing. Nor in any sort of augury is more faith and assurance reposed, not by the populace only, but even by the nobles, even by the Priests. These account themselves the ministers of the Gods, and the horses privy to his will. They have likewise another method of divination, whence to learn the issue of great and mighty wars. From the nation with whom they are at war they contrive, it avails not how, to gain a captive: him they engage in combat with one selected from amongst themselves, each armed after the manner of his country, and according as the victory falls to this or to the other, gather a presage of the whole.

Affairs of smaller moment the chiefs determine: about matters of higher consequence the whole nation deliberates; yet in such sort, that whatever depends upon the pleasure and decision of the people, is examined and discussed by the chiefs. Where no accident or emergency intervenes, they assemble upon stated days, either, when the moon changes, or is full: since they believe such seasons to be the most fortunate for beginning all transactions. Neither in reckoning of time do they count, like us, the number of days but that of nights. In this style their ordinances are framed, in this style their diets appointed; and with them the night seems to lead and govern the day. From their extensive liberty this evil and default flows, that they meet not at once, nor as men commanded and afraid to disobey; so that often the second day, nay often the third, is consumed through the slowness of the members in assembling. They sit down as they list, promiscuously, like a crowd, and all armed. It is by the Priests that silence is enjoined, and with the power of correction the Priests are then invested. Then the King or Chief is heard, as are others, each according to his precedence in age, or in nobility, or in warlike renown, or in eloquence; and the influence of every speaker proceeds rather from his ability to persuade than from any authority to command. If the proposition displease, they reject it by an inarticulate murmur: if it be pleasing, they brandish their javelins. The most honourable manner of signifying their assent, is to express their applause by the sound of their arms.

In the assembly it is allowed to present accusations, and to prosecute capital offences. Punishments vary according to the quality of the crime. Traitors and deserters they hang upon trees. Cowards, and sluggards, and unnatural prostitutes they smother in mud and bogs under an heap of hurdles. Such diversity in their executions has this view, that in punishing of glaring iniquities, it behooves likewise to display them to sight; but effeminacy and pollution must be buried and concealed. In lighter transgressions too the penalty is measured by the fault, and the delinquents upon conviction are condemned to pay a certain number of horses or cattle. Part of this mulct accrues to the King or to the community, part to him whose wrongs are vindicated, or to his next kindred. In the same assemblies are also chosen their chiefs or rulers, such as administer justice in their villages and boroughs. To each of these are assigned an hundred persons chosen from amongst the populace, to accompany and assist him, men who help him at once with their authority and their counsel.

Without being armed they transact nothing, whether of public or private concernment. But it is repugnant to their custom for any man to use arms, before the community has attested his capacity to wield them. Upon such testimonial, either one of the rulers, or his father, or some kinsman dignify the young man in the midst of the assembly, with a shield and javelin. This amongst them is the *manly robe*, this first degree of honour conferred upon their youth. Before this they seem no more than part of a private family, but thenceforward part of the Commonweal. The princely dignity they confer even upon striplings, whose race is eminently noble, or whose fathers have done great and signal services to the State. For about the rest, who are more vigorous and long since tried, they crowd to attend; nor is it any shame to be seen amongst the followers of these. Nay, there are likewise degrees of followers, higher or lower, just as he whom they follow judges fit. Mighty too is the emulation amongst these followers, of each to be first in favour with his Prince; mighty also the emulation of the Princes, to excel in the number and valour of followers. This is their principal state, this their chief force, to be at all times surrounded with a huge band of chosen young men, for ornament and glory in peace, for security and defence in war. Nor is it amongst his own people only, but even from the neighbouring communities, that any of their

Princes reaps so much renown and a name so great, when he surpasses in the number and magnanimity of his followers. For such are courted by Embassies, and distinguished with presents, and by the terror of their fame alone often dissipate wars.

In the day of battle, it is scandalous to the Prince to be surpassed in feats of bravery, scandalous to his followers to fail in matching the bravery of the Prince. But it is infamy during life, and indelible reproach, to return alive from a battle where their Prince was slain. To preserve their Prince, to defend him, and to ascribe to his glory all their own valorous deeds, is the sum and most sacred part of their oath. The Princes fight for victory; for the Prince his followers fight. Many of the young nobility, when their own community comes to languish in its vigour by long peace and inactivity, betake themselves through impatience in other States which then prove to be in war. For, besides that this people cannot brook repose, besides that by perilous adventures they more quickly blazon their fame, they cannot otherwise than by violence and war support their huge train of retainers. For from the liberality of their Prince, they demand and enjoy that *war-horse* of theirs, with that *victorious javelin* dyed in the blood of their enemies. In the place of pay, they are supplied with a daily table and repasts; though grossly prepared, yet very profuse. For maintaining such liberality and munificence, a fund is furnished by continual wars and plunder. Nor could you so easily persuade them to cultivate the ground, or to await the return of the seasons and produce of the year, as to provoke the foe and to risk wounds and death: since stupid and spiritless they account it, to acquire by their sweat what they can gain by their blood.

Upon any recess from war, they do not much attend the chase. Much more of their time they pass in indolence, resigned to sleep and repasts. All the most brave, all the most warlike, apply to nothing at all; but to their wives, to the ancient men, and to even the most impotent domestic, trust all the care of their house, and of their lands and possessions. They themselves loiter. Such is the amazing diversity of their nature, that in the same men is found so much delight in sloth, with so much enmity to tranquillity and repose. The communities are wont, of their own accord and man by man, to bestow upon their Princes a certain number of beasts, or a certain portion of grain; a contribution which passes indeed for a mark of reverence and honour, but serves also to supply their necessities. They chiefly rejoice in the gifts which come from the bordering countries, such as are sent not only by particulars but in the name of the State; curious horses, splendid armour, rich harness, with collars of silver and gold. Now too they have learnt, what we have taught them, to receive money.

That none of the several people in Germany live together in cities, is abundantly known; nay, that amongst them none of their dwellings are suffered to be contiguous. They inhabit apart and distinct, just as a fountain, or a field, or a wood happened to invite them to settle. They raise their villages in opposite rows, but not in our manner with the houses joined one to another. Every man has a vacant space quite round his own, whether for security against accidents from fire, or that they want the art of building. With them in truth, is unknown even the use of mortar and of tiles. In all their structures they employ materials quite gross and unhewn, void of fashion and comeliness. Some parts they besmear with an earth so pure and resplendent, that it resembles painting and colours. They are likewise wont to scoop caves deep in the ground, and over them to lay great heaps of dung. Thither they retire for shelter in the winter, and thither convey their grain: for by such close places they mollify the rigorous and excessive cold. Besides when at any time their enemy invades them, he can only ravage the open country, but either knows not such recesses as are invisible and subterraneous; or must suffer them to escape him, on this very account that he is uncertain where to find them.

For their covering a mantle is what they all wear, fastened with a clasp or, for want of it, with a thorn. As far as this reaches not they are naked, and lie whole days before the fire. The most wealthy are distinguished with a vest, not one large and flowing like those of Sarmatians and Parthians, but girt close about them and expressing the proportion of every limb. They likewise wear the skins of savage beasts, a dress which those bordering upon the Rhine use without any fondness or delicacy, but about which such who live further in the country are more curious, as void of all apparel introduced by commerce. They choose certain wild beasts, and, having flayed them, diversify their hides with many spots, as also with the skins of monsters from the deep, such as are engendered in the distant ocean and in seas unknown. Neither does the dress of the women differ from that of the men, save that the women are orderly attired in linen embroidered with purple, and use no sleeves, so that all their arms are bare. The upper part of their breast is withal exposed.

Yet the laws of matrimony are severely observed there; for in the whole of their manners is aught more praiseworthy than this: for they are almost the only Barbarians contented with one wife, excepting a very few amongst them; men of dignity who marry divers wives, from no wantonness or lubricity, but courted for the lustre of their family into many alliances.

To the husband, the wife tenders no dowry; but the husband, to the wife. The parents and relations attend and declare their approbation of the presents, not presents adapted to feminine pomp and delicacy, nor such as serve to deck the new married woman; but oxen and horse accoutred, and a shield, with a javelin and sword. By virtue of these gifts, she is espoused. She too on her part brings her husband some arms. This they esteem the highest tie, these the holy mysteries, and matrimonial Gods. That the woman may not suppose herself free from the considerations of fortitude and fighting, or exempt from the casualties of war, the very first solemnities of her wedding serve to warn her, that she comes to her husband as a partner in his hazards and fatigues, that she is to suffer alike with him, to adventure alike, during peace or during war. This the oxen joined in the same yoke plainly indicate, this the horse ready equipped, this the present of arms. 'Tis thus she must be content to live, thus to resign life. The arms which she then receives she must preserve inviolate, and to her sons restore the same, as presents worthy of them, such as their wives may again receive, and still resign to her grandchildren.

They therefore live in a state of chastity well secured; corrupted by no seducing shows and public diversions, by no irritations from banqueting. Of learning and of any secret intercourse by letters, they are all equally ignorant, men and women. Amongst a people so numerous, adultery is exceeding rare; a crime instantly punished, and the punishment left to be inflicted by the husband. He, having cut off her hair, expells her from his house naked, in presence of her kindred, and pursues her with stripes throughout the village. For, to a woman who has prostituted her person, no pardon is ever granted. However beautiful she may be, however young, however abounding in wealth, a husband she can never find. In truth, nobody turns vices into mirth there, nor is the practice of corrupting and of yielding to corruption, called the custom of the Age. Better still do those communities, in which none but virgins marry, and where to a single marriage all their views and inclinations are at once confined. Thus, as they have but one body and one life, they take but one husband, that beyond him they may have no thought, no further wishes, nor love him only as their husband but as their marriage. To restrain generation and the increase of children, is esteemed an abominable sin, as also to kill infants newly born. And more powerful with them are good manners, than with other people are good laws.

In all their houses the children are reared naked and nasty; and thus grow into those limbs, into that bulk, which with marvel we behold. They are all nourished with the milk of their own mothers, and never surrendered to handmaids and nurses. The lord you cannot discern from the slave, by any superior delicacy in rearing. Amongst the same cattle they promiscuously live, upon the same ground they without distinction lie, till at a proper age the freeborn are parted from the rest, and their bravery recommend them to notice. Slow and late do the young men come to the use of women, and thus very long preserve the vigour of youth. Neither are the virgins hastened to wed. They must both have the same sprightly youth, the like stature, and marry when equal and able-bodied. Thus the robustness of the parents is inherited by the children. Children are holden in the same estimation with their mother's brother, as with their father. Some hold this tie of blood to be most inviolable and binding, and in receiving of hostages, such pledges are most considered and claimed, as they who at once possess affections the most unalienable, and the most diffuse interest in their family. To every man, however, his own children are heirs and successors: wills they make none: for want of children his next akin inherits; his own brothers, those of his father, or those of his mother. To ancient men, the more they abound in descendants, in relations and affinities, so much the more favour and reverence accrues. From being childless, no advantage nor estimation is derived.

All the enmities of your house, whether of your father or of your kindred, you must necessarily adopt; as well as all their friendships. Neither are such enmities unappeasable and permanent: since even for so great a crime as homicide, compensation is made by a fixed number of sheep and cattle, and by it the whole family is pacified to content. A temper this, wholesome to the State; because to a free nation, animosities and faction are always more menacing and perilous. In social feasts, and deeds of hospitality, no nation upon earth was ever more liberal and abounding. To refuse admitting under your roof any man whatsoever, is held wicked and inhuman. Every man receives every comer, and treats him with repasts as large as his ability can possibly furnish. When the whole stock is consumed, he who has treated so hospitably guides and accompanies his guest to the next house, though neither of them invited. Nor avails it, that they were not; they are there received, with the same frankness and humanity. Between a stranger and an acquaintance, in dispensing the rules and benefits of hospitality, no difference is made. Upon your departure, if you ask anything, it is the custom to grant it; and with the same facility, they ask of you. In gifts they delight, but neither claim merit from what they give, nor own any obligation for what they receive. Their manner of entertaining their guests is familiar and kind.

The moment they rise from sleep, which they generally prolong till late in the day, they bathe, most frequently in warm water; as in a country where the winter is very long and severe. From bathing, they sit down to meat; every man apart, upon a particular seat, and at a separate table. They then proceed to their affairs, all in arms; as in arms, they no less frequently go to banquet. To continue drinking night and day without intermission, is a reproach to no man. Frequent then are their broils, as usual amongst men intoxicated with liquor; and such broils rarely terminate in angry words, but for the most part in maimings and slaughter. Moreover in these their feasts, they generally deliberate about reconciling parties at enmity, about forming affinities, choosing of Princes, and finally about peace and war. For they judge, that at no season is the soul more open to thoughts that are artless and upright, or more fired with such as are great and bold. This people, of themselves nowise subtile or politic, from the freedom of the place and occasion acquire still more frankness to disclose the most secret motions and purposes of their hearts. When therefore the minds of all have been once laid open and declared, on the day following the several sentiments are revised and canvassed; and to both conjectures of time, due regard is had. They consult, when they know not how to dissemble; they determine, when they cannot mistake.

For their drink, they draw a liquor from barley or other grain; and ferment the same so as to make it resemble wine. Nay, they who dwell upon the bank of the Rhine deal in wine. Their food is very simple; wild fruit, fresh venison, or coagulated milk. They banish hunger without formality, without curious dressing and curious fare. In extinguishing thirst, they use not equal temperance. If you will but humour their excess in drinking, and supply them with as much as they covet, it will be no less easy to vanquish them by vices than by arms.

Of public diversions they have but one sort, and in all their meetings the same is still exhibited. Young men, such as make it their pastime, fling themselves naked and dance amongst sharp swords and the deadly points of javelins. From habit they acquire their skill, and from their skill a graceful manner; yet from hence draw no gain or hire: though this adventurous gaiety has its reward, namely, that of pleasing the spectators. What is marvellous, playing at dice is one of their most serious employments; and even sober, they are gamesters: nay, so desperately do they venture upon the chance of winning or losing, that when their whole substance is played away, they stake their liberty and their persons upon one and the last throw. The loser goes calmly into voluntary bondage. However younger he be, however stronger, he tamely suffers himself to be bound and sold by the winner. Such is their perseverance in an evil course: they themselves call it honour.

Slaves of this class, they exchange in commerce, to free themselves too from the shame of such a victory. Of their other slaves they make not such use as we do of ours, by distributing amongst them the several offices and employments of the family. Each of them has a dwelling of his own, each a household to govern. His lord uses him like a tenant, and obliges him to pay a quantity of grain, or of cattle, or of cloth. Thus far only the subserviency of the slave extends. All the other duties in a family, not the slaves, but the wives and children discharge. To inflict stripes upon a slave, or to put him in chains, or to doom him to severe labour, are things rarely seen. To kill them they sometimes are wont, not through correction or government, but in heat and rage, as they would an enemy, save that no vengeance or penalty follows. The freedmen very little surpass the slaves, rarely are of moment in the house; in the community never, excepting only such nations where arbitrary dominion prevails. For there they bear higher sway than the free-born, nay, higher than the nobles. In other countries the inferior condition of freedmen is a proof of public liberty.

To the practice of usury and of increasing money by interest, they are strangers; and hence is found a better guard against it, than if it were forbidden. They shift from land to land; and, still appropriating a portion suitable to the number of hands for manuring, anon parcel out the whole amongst particulars according to the condition and quality of each. As the plains are very spacious, the allotments are easily assigned. Every year they change, and cultivate a fresh soil; yet still there is ground to spare. For they strive not to bestow labour proportionable to the fertility and compass of their lands, by planting orchards, by enclosing meadows, by watering gardens. From the earth, corn only is extracted. Hence they quarter not the year into so many seasons. Winter, Spring, and Summer, they understand; and for each have proper appellations. Of the name and blessings of Autumn, they are equally ignorant.

In performing their funerals, they show no state or vainglory. This only is carefully observed, that with the corpses of their signal men certain woods be burned. Upon the funeral pile they accumulate neither apparel nor perfumes. Into the fire, are always thrown the arms of the dead, and sometimes his horse. With sods of earth only the sepulchre is raised. The pomp of tedious and elaborate monuments they contemn, as things grievous to the deceased. Tears and wailings they soon dismiss: their affliction and woe they long retain. In women, it is reckoned becoming to bewail their loss; in men, to remember it. This is what in general we have learned, in the original and customs of the whole people of Germany. I shall now deduce the institutions and usages of the several people, as far as they vary one from another; as also an account of what nations from thence removed, to settle themselves in Gaul.

That the Gauls were in times past more puissant and formidable, is related by the Prince of authors, the deified Julius [Caesar]; and hence it is probable that they too have passed into Germany. For what a small obstacle must be a river, to restrain any nation, as each grew more potent, from seizing or changing habitations; when as yet all habitations were common, and not parted or appropriated by the founding and terror of Monarchies? The region therefore between the Hercynian Forest and the rivers Moenus and Rhine, was occupied by the Helvetians; as was that beyond it by the Boians, both nations of Gaul. There still remains a place called *Boiemum*, which denotes the primitive name and antiquity of the country, although the inhabitants have been changed. But whether the Araviscans are derived from the Osians, a nation of Germans passing into Pannonia, or the Osians from the Araviscans removing from thence into Germany, is a matter undecided; since they both still use the language, the same customs and the same laws. For, as of old they lived alike poor and alike free, equal proved the evils and advantages on each side the river, and common to both people. The Treverians and Nervians aspire passionately to the reputation of being descended from the Germans; since by the glory of this original, they would escape all imputation of resembling the Gauls in person and effeminacy. Such as dwell upon the bank of the Rhine, the Vangiones, the Tribocians, and the Nemetes, are without doubt all Germans. The Ubians are ashamed of their original; though they have a particular honour to boast, that of having merited an establishment as a Roman Colony, and still delight to be called *Agrippinensians*, after the name of their founder: they indeed formerly came from beyond the Rhine, and, for the many proofs of their fidelity, were settled upon the very bank of the river; not to be there confined or guarded themselves, but to guard and defend that boundary against the rest of the Germans.

Of all these nations, the Batavians are the most signal in bravery. They inhabit not much territory upon the Rhine, but possess an island in it. They were formerly part of the Cattans, and by means of feuds at home removed to these dwellings; whence they might become a portion of the Roman Empire. With them this honour still remains, as also the memorials of their ancient association with us: for they are not under the contempt of paying tribute, nor subject to be squeezed by the farmers of the revenue. Free from all impositions and payments, and only set apart for the purposes of fighting, they are reserved wholly for the wars, in the same manner as a magazine of weapons and armour. Under the same degree of homage are the nation of the Mattiacians. For such is the might and greatness of the Roman People, as to have carried the awe and esteem of their Empire beyond the Rhine and the ancient boundaries. Thus the Mattiacians, living upon the opposite banks, enjoy a settlement and limits of their own; yet in spirit and inclination are attached to us: in other things resembling the Batavians, save that as they still breathe their original air, still possess their primitive soil, they are thence inspired with superior vigour and keenness. Amongst the people of Germany I would not reckon those who occupy the lands which are under decimation, though they be such as dwell beyond the Rhine and the Danube. By several worthless and vagabond Gauls, and such as poverty rendered daring, that region was seized as one belonging to no certain possessor: afterwards it became a skirt of the Empire and part of a province, upon the enlargement of our bounds and the extending of our garrisons and frontier.

Beyond these are the Cattans, whose territories begin at the Hercynian Forest, and consist not of such wide and marshy plains, as those of the other communities contained within the vast compass of Germany; but produce ranges of hills, such as run lofty and contiguous for a long tract, then by degrees sink and decay. Moreover the Hercynian Forest attends for a while its native Cattans, then suddenly forsakes them. This people are distinguished with bodies more hardy and robust, compact limbs, stern countenances, and greater vigour of spirit. For Germans, they are men of much sense and address. They dignify chosen men, listen to such as are set over them, know how to preserve their post, to discern occasions, to rebate their own ardour and impatience; how to employ the day, how to entrench themselves by night. They account fortune amongst things slippery and uncertain, but bravery amongst such as are never-failing and secure; and, what is exceeding rare nor ever to be learnt but by a wholesome course of discipline, in the conduct of the general they repose more assurance than in the strength of the army. Their whole forces consist of foot, who besides their arms carry likewise instruments of iron and their provisions. You may see other Germans proceed equipped to battle, but the Cattans so as to conduct a war. They rarely venture upon excursions or casual encounters. It is in truth peculiar to cavalry, suddenly to conquer, or suddenly to fly. Such haste and velocity rather resembles fear. Patience and deliberation are more akin to intrepidity.

Moreover a custom, practised indeed in other nations of Germany, yet very rarely and confined only to particulars more daring than the rest, prevails amongst the Cattans by universal consent. As soon as they arrive to maturity of years, they let their hair and beards continue to grow, nor till they have slain an enemy do they ever lay aside this form of countenance by vow sacred to valour. Over the blood and spoil of a foe they make bare their face. They allege, that they have now acquitted themselves of the debt and duty contracted by their birth, and rendered themselves worthy of their country, worthy of their parents. Upon the spiritless, cowardly and unwarlike, such deformity of visage still remains. All the most brave likewise wear an iron ring (a mark of great dishonour this in that nation) and retain it as a chain; till by killing an enemy they become released. Many of the Cattans delight always to bear this terrible aspect; and, when grown white through age, become awful and conspicuous by such marks, both to the enemy and their own countrymen. By them in all engagements the first assault is made: of them the front of the battle is always composed, as men who in their looks are singular and tremendous. For even during peace they abate nothing in the grimness and horror of their countenance. They have no house to inhabit, no land to cultivate, nor any domestic charge or care. With whomsoever they come to sojourn, by him they are maintained; always very prodigal of the substance of others, always despising what is their own, till the feebleness of old age overtakes them, and renders them unequal to the efforts of such rigid bravery.

Next to the Cattans, dwell the Usipians and Tencterians; upon the Rhine now running in a channel uniform and certain, such as suffices for a boundary. The Tencterians, besides their wonted glory in war, surpass in the service and discipline of their cavalry. Nor do the Cattans derive higher applause from their foot, than the Tencterians from their horse. Such was the order established by their forefathers, and what their posterity still pursue. From riding and exercising of horse, their children borrow their pastimes; in this exercise the young men find matter for emulating one another, and in this the old men take pleasure to persevere. Horses are by the father bequeathed as part of his household and family, horses are conveyed amongst the rights of succession, and as such the son receives them; but not the eldest son, like other effects, by priority of birth, but he who continues to be signal in boldness and superior in war.

Contiguous to the Tencterians formerly dwelt the Bructerians, in whose room it is said the Chamavians and Angrivarians are now settled; they who expulsed and almost extirpated the Bructerians, with the concurrence of the neighbouring nations: whether in detestation of their arrogance, or allured by the love of spoil, or through the special favour of the Gods towards us Romans. They in truth even vouchsafed to gratify us with the sight of the battle. In it there fell above sixty thousand souls, without a blow struck by the Romans; but, what is a circumstance still more glorious, fell to furnish them with a spectacle of joy and recreation. May the Gods continue and perpetuate amongst these nations, if not any love for us, yet by all means this their animosity and hate towards each other: since whilst the destiny of the Empire thus urges it, fortune cannot more signally befriend us, than in sowing strife amongst our foes.

The Angrivarians and Chamavians are enclosed behind, by the Dulgibinians and Chasuarians; and by other nations not so much noted: before the Frisians face them. The country of Frisia is divided into two; called the greater and lesser, according to the measure of their strength. Both nations stretch along the Rhine, quite to the ocean; and surround vast lakes such as once have born Roman fleets. We have moreover even ventured out from thence into the ocean, and upon its coasts common fame has reported the pillars of Hercules to be still standing: whether it be that Hercules ever visited these parts, or that to his renowned name we are wont to ascribe whatever is grand and glorious everywhere. Neither did Drusus who made the attempt, want boldness to pursue it: but the roughness of the ocean withstood him, nor would suffer discoveries to be made about itself, no more than about Hercules. Thenceforward the enterprise was dropped: nay, more pious and reverential it seemed, to believe the marvellous feats of the Gods than to know and to prove them.

Hitherto, I have been describing Germany towards the west. To the northward, it winds away with an immense compass. And first of all occurs the nation of the Chaucians; who though they begin immediately at the confines of the Frisians, and occupy part of the shore, extend so far as to border upon all the several people whom I have already recounted; till at last, by a Circuit, they reach quite to the boundaries of the Cattans. A region so vast, the Chaucians do not only possess but fill; a people of all the Germans the most noble, such as would rather maintain their grandeur by justice than violence. They live in repose, retired from broils abroad, void of avidity to possess more, free from a spirit of domineering over others. They provoke no wars, they ravage no countries, they pursue no plunder. Of their bravery and power, the chief evidence arises from hence, that, without wronging or oppressing others, they are come to be superior to all. Yet they are all ready to arm, and if an exigency require, armies are presently raised, powerful and abounding as they are in men and horses; and even when they are quiet and their weapons laid aside, their credit and name continue equally high.

Along the side of the Chaucians and Cattans dwell the Cheruscans; a people who finding no enemy to rouse them, were enfeebled by a peace over lasting and uniform, but such as they failed not to nourish. A conduct which proved more pleasing than secure; since treacherous is that repose which you enjoy amongst neighbours that are very powerful and very fond of rule and mastership. When recourse is once had to the sword, modesty and fair dealing will be vainly pleaded by the weaker; names these which are always assumed by the stronger. Thus the Cheruscans, they who formerly bore the character of *good and upright*, are now called *cowards and fools*; and the fortune of the Cattans who subdued them, grew immediately to be wisdom. In the ruin of the Cheruscans, the Fosians, also their neighbours, were involved; and in their calamities bore an equal share, though in their prosperity they had been weaker and less considered.

In the same winding tract of Germany live the Cimbrians, close to the ocean; a community now very small, but great in fame. Nay, of their ancient renown, many and extensive are the traces and monuments still remaining; even their entrenchments upon either shore, so vast in compass that from thence you may even now measure the greatness and numerous bands of that people, and assent to the account of an army so mighty. It was on the six hundred and fortieth year of Rome, when of the arms of the Cimbrians the first mention was made, during the Consulship of Caecilius Metellus and Papirius Carbo. If from that time we count to the second Consulship of the Emperor Trajan, the interval comprehends near two hundred and ten years; so long have we been conquering Germany. In a course of time, so vast between these two periods, many have been the blows and disasters suffered on each side. In truth neither from the Samnites, nor from the Carthaginians, nor from both Spains, nor from all the nations of Gaul, have we received more frequent checks and alarms; nor even from the Parthians: for, more vigorous and invincible is the liberty of the Germans than the monarchy of the Arsacides. Indeed, what has the power of the East to allege to our dishonour; but the fall of Crassus, that power which was itself overthrown and abased by Ventidius, with the loss of the great King Pacorus bereft of his life? But by the Germans the Roman People have been bereft of five armies, all commanded by Consuls; by the Germans, the commanders of these armies, Carbo, and Cassius, and Scaurus Aurelius, and Servilius Caepio, as also Marcus Manlius, were all routed or taken: by the Germans even the Emperor Augustus was bereft of Varus and three legions. Nor without difficulty and loss of men were they defeated by Caius Marius in Italy, or by the deified Julius in Gaul, or by Drusus or Tiberius or Germanicus in their native territories. Soon after, the mighty menaces of Caligula against them ended in mockery and derision. Thenceforward they continued quiet, till taking advantage of our domestic division and civil wars, they stormed and seized the winter entrenchments of the legions, and aimed at the dominion of Gaul; from whence they were once more expelled, and in the times preceding the present, we gained a triumph over them rather than a victory.

I must now proceed to speak of the Suevians, who are not, like the Cattans and Tencterians, comprehended in a single people; but divided into several nations all bearing distinct names, though in general they are entitled Suevians, and occupy the larger share of Germany. This people are remarkable for a peculiar custom, that of twisting their hair and binding it up in a knot. It is thus the Suevians are distinguished from the other Germans, thus the free Suevians from their slaves. In other nations, whether from alliance of blood with the Suevians, or, as is usual from imitation, this practice is also found, yet rarely, and never exceeds the years of youth. The Suevians, even when their hair is white through age, continue to raise it backwards in a manner stern and staring; and often tie it upon the top of their head only. That of their Princes, is more accurately disposed, and so far they study to appear agreeable and comely; but without any culpable intention. For by it, they mean not to make love or to incite it: they thus dress when proceeding to war, and deck their heads so as to add to their height and terror in the eyes of the enemy.

Of all the Suevians, the Semnones recount themselves to be the most ancient and most noble. The belief of their antiquity is confirmed by religious mysteries. At a stated time of the year, all the several people descended from the same stock, assemble by their deputies in a wood; consecrated by the idolatries of their forefathers, and by superstitious awe in times of old. There by publicly sacrificing a man, they begin the horrible solemnity of their barbarous worship. To this grove another sort of reverence is also paid. No one enters it otherwise than bound with ligatures, thence professing his subordination and meanness, and power of the Deity there. If he fall down, he is not permitted to rise or be raised, but grovels along upon the ground. And of all their superstition, this is the drift and tendency; that from this place the nation drew their original, that here God, the supreme Governor of the world, resides, and that all things else whatsoever are subject to him and bound to obey him. The potent condition of the Semnones has increased their influence and authority, as they inhabit an hundred towns; and from the largeness of their community it comes, that they hold themselves for the head of the Suevians.

What on the contrary ennobles the Langobards is the smallness of their number, for that they, who are surrounded with very many and very powerful nations, derive their security from no obsequiousness or plying; but from the dint of battle and adventurous deeds. There follow in order the Reudignians, and Aviones, and Angles, and Varinians, and Eudoses, and Suardones and Nuithones; all defended by rivers or forests. Nor in one of these nations does aught remarkable occur, only that they universally join in the worship of *Herthum*; that is to say, the Mother Earth. Her they believe to interpose in the affairs of men, and to visit countries. In an island of the ocean stands the wood *Castum*: in it is a chariot dedicated to the Goddess covered over with a curtain, and permitted to be touched by none but the Priest. Whenever the Goddess enters this her holy vehicle, he perceives her; and with profound veneration attends the motion of the chariot, which is always drawn by yoked cows. Then it is that days of rejoicing always ensue, and in all places whatsoever which she descends to honour with a visit and her company, feasts and recreation abound. They go not to war; they touch no arms; fast laid up is every hostile weapon; peace and repose are then only known, then only beloved, till to the temple the same priest reconducts the Goddess when well tired with the conversation of mortal beings. Anon the chariot is washed and purified in a secret lake, as also the curtain; nay, the Deity herself too, if you choose to believe it. In this office it is slaves who minister, and they are forthwith doomed to be swallowed up in the same lake. Hence all men are possessed with mysterious terror; as well as with a holy ignorance what that must be, which none see but such as are immediately to perish. Moreover this quarter of the Suevians stretches to the middle of Germany.

The community next adjoining, is that of the Hermondurians; (that I may now follow the course of the Danube, as a little before I did that of the Rhine) a people this, faithful to the Romans. So that to them alone of all the Germans, commerce is permitted; not barely upon the bank of the Rhine, but more extensively, and even in that glorious colony in the province of Rhoetia. They travel everywhere at their own discretion and without a guard; and when to other nations, we show no more than our arms and encampments, to this people we throw open our houses and dwellings, as to men who have no longing to possess them. In the territories of the Hermondurians rises the Elbe, a river very famous and formerly well known to us; at present we only hear it named.

Close by the Hermondurians reside the Nariscans, and next to them the Marcomanians and Quadians. Amongst these the Marcomanians are most signal in force and renown; nay, their habitation itself they acquired by their bravery, as from thence they formerly expulsed the Boians. Nor do the Nariscans or Quadians degenerate in spirit. Now this is as it were the frontier of Germany, as far as Germany is washed by the Danube. To the times within our memory the Marcomanians and Quadians were governed by kings, who were natives of their own, descended from the noble line of Maroboduus and Tudrus. At present they are even subject to such as are foreigners. But the whole strength and sway of their king is derived from the authority of the Romans. From our arms, they rarely receive any aid; from our money very frequently.

Nor less powerful are the several people beyond them; namely, the Marsignians, the Gothinians, the Osians and the Burians, who altogether enclose the Marcomanians and Quadians behind. Of those, the Marsignians and the Burians in speech and dress resemble the Suevians. From the Gallic language spoken by the Gothinians, and from that of Pannonia by the Osians, it is manifest that neither of these people are Germans; as it is also from their bearing to pay tribute. Upon them as upon aliens their tribute is imposed, partly by the Sarmatians, partly by the Quadians. The Gothinians, to heighten their disgrace, are forced to labour in the iron mines. By all these several nations but little level country is possessed: they are seated amongst forests, and upon the ridges and declivities of mountains. For, Suevia is parted by a continual ridge of mountains; beyond which, live many distinct nations. Of these the Lygians are most numerous and extensive, and spread into several communities. It will suffice to mention the most puissant; even the Arians,

Helvicones, Manimians; Elysians and Naharvalians. Amongst the Naharvalians is shown a grove, sacred to devotion extremely ancient. Over it a Priest presides apparelled like a woman; but according to the explication of the Romans, 'tis *Castor* and *Pollux* who are here worshipped. This Divinity is named *Alcis*. There are indeed no images here, no traces of an extraneous superstition; yet their devotion is addressed to young men and to brothers. Now the Arians, besides their forces, in which they surpass the several nations just recounted, are in their persons stern and truculent; and even humour and improve their natural grimness and ferocity by art and time. They wear black shields, their bodies are painted black, they choose dark nights for engaging in battle; and by the very awe and ghastly hue of their army, strike the enemy with dread, as none can bear this their aspect so surprising and as it were quite infernal. For, in all battles the eyes are vanquished first.

Beyond the Lygians dwell the Gothones, under the rule of a King; and thence held in subjection somewhat stricter than the other German nations, yet not so strict as to extinguish all their liberty. Immediately adjoining are the Rugians and Lemovians upon the coast of the ocean, and of these several nations the characteristics are a round shield, a short sword and kingly government. Next occur the communities of the Suiones, situated in the ocean itself; and besides their strength in men and arms, very powerful at sea. The form of their vessels varies thus far from ours, that they have prows at each end, so as to be always ready to row to shore without turning nor are they moved by sails, nor on their sides have benches of oars placed, but the rowers ply here and there in all parts of the ship alike, as in some rivers is done, and change their oars from place to place, just as they shift their course hither or thither. To wealth also, amongst them, great veneration is paid, and thence a single ruler governs them, without all restriction of power, and exacting unlimited obedience. Neither here, as amongst other nations of Germany, are arms used indifferently by all, but shut up and warded under the care of a particular keeper, who in truth too is always a slave: since from all sudden invasions and attacks from their foes, the ocean protects them: besides that armed bands, when they are not employed, grow easily debauched and tumultuous. The truth is, it suits not the interest of an arbitrary Prince, to trust the care and power of arms either with a nobleman or with a freeman, or indeed with any man above the condition of a slave.

Beyond the Suiones is another sea, one very heavy and almost void of agitation; and by it the whole globe is thought to be bounded and environed, for that the reflection of the sun, after his setting, continues till his rising, so bright as to darken the stars. To this, popular opinion has added, that the tumult also of his emerging from the sea is heard, that forms divine are then seen, as likewise the rays about his head. Only thus far extend the limits of nature, if what fame says be true. Upon the right of the Suevian Sea the AEstyan nations reside, who use the same customs and attire with the Suevians; their language more resembles that of Britain. They worship the Mother of the Gods. As the characteristic of their national superstition, they wear the images of wild boars. This alone serves them for arms, this is the safeguard of all, and by this every worshipper of the goddess is secured even amidst his foes. Rare amongst them is the use of weapons of iron, but frequent that of clubs. In producing of grain and the other fruits of the earth, they labour with more assiduity and patience than is suitable to the usual laziness of Germans. Nay, they even search the deep, and of all the rest are the only people who gather *amber*. They call it *glasing*, and find it amongst the shallows and upon the very shore. But, according to the ordinary incuriosity and ignorance of Barbarians, they have neither learnt, nor do they inquire, what is its nature, or from what cause it is produced. In truth it lay long neglected amongst the other gross discharges of the sea; till from our luxury, it gained a name and value. To themselves it is of no use: they gather it rough, they expose it in pieces coarse and unpolished, and for it receive a price with wonder. You would however conceive it to be a liquor issuing from trees, for that in the transparent substance are often seen birds and other animals, such as at first stuck in the soft gum, and by it, as it hardened, became quite enclosed. I am apt to believe that, as in the recesses of the East are found woods and groves dropping frankincense and balms, so in the isles and continent of the West such gums are extracted by the force and proximity of the sun; at first liquid and flowing into the next sea, then thrown by the winds and waves upon the opposite shore. If you try the nature of amber by the application of fire, it kindles like a torch; and feeds a thick and unctuous flame very high scented, and presently becomes glutinous like pitch or rosin.

Upon the Suiones, border the people Sitones; and, agreeing with them in all other things, differ from them in one, that here the sovereignty is exercised by a woman. So notoriously do they degenerate not only from a state of liberty, but even below a state of bondage. Here end the territories of the Suevians.

Whether amongst the Sarmatians or the Germans I ought to account the Peucinians, the Venedians, and the Fennians, is what I cannot determine; though the Peucinians, whom some call Basstarnians, speak the same language with the Germans, use the same attire, build like them, and live like them, in that dirtiness and sloth so common to all. Somewhat they are corrupted into the fashion of the Sarmatians by the inter-marriages of the principal sort with that nation: from whence the Venedians have derived very many of their customs and a great resemblance. For they are continually traversing and infesting with robberies all the forests and mountains lying between the Peucinians and Fennians. Yet they are rather reckoned amongst the Germans, for that they have fixed houses, and carry shields, and prefer travelling on foot, and excel in swiftness. Usages these, all widely differing from those of the Sarmatians, who live on horseback and dwell in waggons. In wonderful savageness live the nation of the Fennians, and in beastly poverty, destitute of arms, of horses, and of homes; their food, the common herbs; their apparel, skins; their bed, the earth; their only hope in their arrows, which for want of iron they point with bones. Their common support they have from the chase, women as well as men; for with these the former wander up and down, and crave a portion of the prey. Nor other shelter have they even for their babes, against the violence of tempests and ravening beasts, than to cover them with the branches of trees twisted together; this a reception for the old men, and hither resort the young. Such a condition they judge more happy than the painful occupation of cultivating the ground, than the labour of rearing houses, than the agitations of hope and fear attending the defence of their own property or the seizing that of others. Secure against the designs of men, secure against the malignity of the Gods, they have accomplished a thing of infinite difficulty; that to them nothing remains even to be wished.

What further accounts we have are fabulous: as that the Hellusians and Oxiones have the countenances and aspect of men, with the bodies and limbs of savage beasts. This, as a thing about which I have no certain information, I shall leave untouched.